MW00512586

THE CHASE STUDY GUIDE

"With clear, honest, and precise writing, Mario Busacca and Hoyt Byrum have created a work capturing our shared quest for purpose, belonging, and a higher union. *The Chase* embraces these central issues in a narrative that is simple enough to be accessible and layered enough to probe the deeper questions that define spirituality. This is a book to read more than once, and slowly, so that these questions might take proper root."

—Greg Fields, Author, *Through the Waters and the Wild*

"*The Chase* is an engaging and relatable book with valuable takeaways for us all. Told in story format, it will capture the reader's attention and expand their perspectives on what it means to be a Christian. The accompanying study guide will ensure that facilitators can easily lead small group discussions that are productive and meaningful. Kudos to Busacca and Byrum for making biblical concepts accessible and for introducing a model we can all follow in our complex modern world."

—Linda Cobb, President, The Coaching Company, Inc.

"I was drawn into the story of Tony, and even though I was brought up in a Christian home, I 'got' his position. And as the story unfolded, I was there like a fly on the wall, waiting to see what happened next. As a believer, I wasn't sure how this was going to relate to me . . . and then . . . there was an explanation of the parable of the Prodigal Son. Wow. Just wow. The insights. I do believe that this is a compelling story for non-believers to get an introduction—and even more so for Believers, whose beliefs may be strong, or not. There's something here for everyone to learn."

—Dr. Sony Jackson, President, Marketing Tools for Coaches

"If you ever feel like you're running all the time with no finish line in sight, pick up *The Chase* and receive hope for your journey. A warm and encouraging spiritual novel about how God has a plan for each of us and works through ordinary people, through the joys and sorrows of everyday life. A terrific book and study guide for small groups or church book clubs."

—Judy Christie, Author of Eighteen Books, Including the Gone to Green Series

"As a pastor who was always looking for creative ways to communicate the essence of the Christian life to those within my congregation, *The Chase* is a resource I welcome. *The Chase* is a unique book in that it is on the one hand a novel worthy of reading simply for pleasure. It is, however, much more than that. It is a book that takes the reader into the most important topics needing to be examined for those who want to embrace the Christian life to the fullest. It presents the good news of the Gospel and it leads the reader into deep discipleship. *The Study Guide* for small groups or book clubs is brilliant."

—Reverend Bill Anderson, Honorably Retired Presbyterian Church (USA) Pastor

"The story of *The Chase* has a marvelous way of pulling you in and allowing you to share the complex feelings of a man on a journey of discovery and a life-changing encounter with the Lord who loves him."

—E. Stanley Ott, Founder & President Vital Churches Institute

"I read tons of books each year and *The Chase* had me riveted to the story from the first chapter on. I loved how the key themes of God's grace and our resulting gratitude and generosity were illustrated by life examples and relationships. I was impressed by the quality of the unique study guide that accompanied this novel.

"*The Chase* book and study guide are tremendous resources for an existing or newly formed small group in a local church, in a neighborhood, or on a college campus. Spiritual seekers as well as growing disciples will benefit greatly from this book and will find themselves growing closer in their relationship with God."

—Bob Reusser, Veteran Navigator Staff, Founder and Former Director of the Navigators Encore Mission

"*The Chase* is a wonderful gift to Kingdom work! For seekers, it is a companionable walk; for believers, it is a thought-twisting serendipitous journey."

—Kathy Turner, librarian emerita

The Chase Study Guide

by Mario Busacca and Hoyt A. Byrum

Published by

 köehlerbooks™

3705 Shore Drive
Virginia Beach, VA 23455
800-435-4811
www.koehlerbooks.com

THE
CHASE
STUDY GUIDE

Where Grace, Gratitude
& Generosity Intersect

REVEALING THE 3G LIFESTYLE
FOR THE CHRISTIAN LIFE

MARIO BUSACCA & HOYT A. BYRUM

VIRGINIA BEACH
CAPE CHARLES

TABLE OF CONTENTS

INTRODUCTION

Tony Hunter is a "work in progress." We meet him in his early thirties, but the person we see has been living with his wounds since childhood. His mother died of cancer when he was a teen, so his father, Tom, did the best he could raising Tony as a single parent.

Tony has been soured on religion. Soured, how? Tom has raised him to reject the idea that there is a God, distrust the church, become skeptical of every "do-gooder," and trust in few others. His philosophy is that no one does anything for someone else unless there is something in it for themselves. Tom's not a bad guy. He is just a man who never recovered from the loss of his wife, and he resisted receiving any support from those who had come from the church to be with his wife when she was sick. Because his wife died in spite of all the prayers offered for her healing, his heart hardened to religion and religious people.

The Chase is a chronicle of how Tony works through his doubts about God, ultimately experiencing freedom for a new and invigorating way of life. Central to his journey are key relationships: his wife Beth, his best friends Dave and Sarah, and Pastor Bob. Each of these main characters listened to Tony, accepted Tony as he was, and believed that God would draw Tony into a new and life-changing relationship if they just remained patient. Perhaps most importantly, they "spoke the truth in love" to Tony, trusting that the truth would not push Tony away but would bring God's perspective to his damaged heart.

This Study Guide is written for members of small groups who come together to experience what Tony experienced: friends who will accept you as you are; friends who will listen to your story with no judgment; friends who will respond to you with truth and love.

Those are the keys for meaningful small group interaction: Acceptance, Truth, Love.

The Chase is not the "Gospel Lite." It is deep discipleship in story form. It is an adventure that will, hopefully, cause you to deepen your relationship with God. Enjoy spending time with other group members as together you watch your lives change for the better.

STUDY GUIDE FACILITATION NOTES

This Study Guide is designed to help generate discussion among group members. The group facilitators are responsible for helping guide these discussions. As such, the facilitators are not expected to be "teachers." They do not need to be experts in the Bible or in biblical teaching. Rather, they should focus on how to draw out the group members by sharing their views and thoughts. The following are some notes on how to accomplish active discussion and interaction.

PREPARATION

Facilitators must have read the week's material prior to the meeting. They must also answer all the questions in the Study Guide from their own perspective. As the members are asked to be open and honest, so should the facilitator. The facilitator, when focusing on a particular verse(s) quoted in the Study Guide, may want to read from their own translation as well as the surrounding verses to further develop the context of the scriptures discussed. This information can then be used to stimulate discussion during the meeting.

The Study Guide uses the English Standard Version (ESV) translation. However, it does not matter what Bible version you use.

In fact, having different versions can be a good discussion vehicle, as different translations can bring additional insights into what the writer is emphasizing.

IMPLEMENTATION

During small group meetings, groups will look to the facilitators to guide the discussion. The key is for the facilitators to say as little as possible. The more they speak, the less the group shares. Based on their preparation, they may share some of their own insights and answers to the questions to get things going. This can demonstrate a level of vulnerability in the facilitators which says to the group members, *I can trust you with what I am thinking and so can you trust me.* However, facilitators should not make statements that imply that their view is the only one worthy of consideration. Although there are right and wrong answers to what the Bible teaches, such as "Salvation is based on God's grace, not our human efforts," there are no incorrect or wrong responses to the questions posed in the Study Guide in terms of each person's experience and belief at this point in their lives.

In addition, facilitators may wish to prepare their own questions; ones that may have arisen in their own minds as they read the material. These can be used during the discussion when it appears that no one is willing to share regarding the Study Guide questions or the discussion on those questions has run its course.

One of the hardest things for facilitators to do is to ensure that everyone has had a chance to contribute to the discussion. Some people may be shy and reluctant to share their thoughts because they think that what they have to say is wrong, or they feel it does not have any value, or they simply want to keep their thoughts and ideas to themselves. Introverts process internally, not by speaking. Facilitators should watch for this and encourage those people to share. On the other hand, there may be members of the group who tend to dominate the conversation. Extroverts think by talking things through out loud. Facilitators can address this by thanking them for their input and then asking someone else to share. This is a delicate balance but can be managed with some experience over time. It is also important to establish early that anything that is shared during the meetings is to be held in confidence by the group members.

Please be respectful of peoples' time. Establish the start and end times for your meetings and honor them. Ensure that you meet in a place that is free of distractions. Food always makes for a more congenial environment. If appropriate, have snacks and drinks available for the group. However, it should not be the facilitator's sole responsibility to provide food. Group members are usually happy to bring the snacks. Ask the group if and how they want to handle this, and you may find that you have many volunteers. Keep the food as simple as possible so you don't get into a competition among the group members for who makes the snacks the most lavish.

PRAYER REQUESTS

The last item in each session is prayer requests. Again, facilitators should prompt the group members to voice their own requests and needs. The Study Guide also suggests that there be a closing prayer(s). The group may look to facilitators to offer a closing prayer. However, it is recommended facilitators encourage others to pray as well. The group may also choose to open each session with prayer. It may be appropriate to have this responsibility rotate for each session, thereby giving those who are comfortable praying out loud, the opportunity. There is no hard and fast rule regarding this; each group is different. However, do not make the mistake of "forcing" someone to pray out loud. This can be a big turn off and should be avoided.

CLOSING

Each session has an action step for the members of the group to implement. These are very important, as actions are integral to accomplishing true life changes. In closing each session, facilitators should review the action step in the Study Guide and actively encourage the members to consider their individual action step.

FINAL NOTE

The focus of the study is to learn, from the readings and from each other, and to have an enjoyable experience. If successful, the group will come closer together and bond in ways that they did not expect when they started. So relax and have fun with it. The more enjoyable the group sessions are for the facilitators, the more enjoyable they will be for the group members as well.

KNOCK, KNOCK, MAY I COME IN?

GETTING TO KNOW EACH OTHER
CHAPTERS 1-12

To be loved but not known is comforting but superficial. To be known and not loved is our greatest fear. But to be fully known and truly loved is, well, a lot like being loved by God. It is what we need more than anything. It liberates us from pretense, humbles us out of our self-righteousness. And fortifies us for any difficulty life can throw at us.

—TIMOTHY KELLER, **founding pastor of Redeemer Presbyterian Church**

THIS SESSION

The Chase doesn't waste any time letting you know that Tony is human. We learn early that Tony is hurting from being passed over for a promotion at his place of work. Not only is he upset at this latest rejection, Tony is also still hurting over a missed promotion from his earlier times in the Armed Forces.

Things aren't all that great at home either. In the first chapter of *The Chase*, we see a divide between Tony and his wife Beth over the timing for having children. Tony claims he wants children but just not now. Beth is tired of waiting and she makes that very clear to Tony. The tension between them is difficult for both.

Maybe the most challenging part of Tony's life, however, is his attempt to live life without a spiritual center. Since he doesn't believe there is a God, naturally he doesn't try to draw comfort, strength, courage, or meaning for life from God. And he is completely turned off by the church and is skeptical regarding followers of Christ. As Tony told Dave, "The church did nothing for me or my family when we most needed it."

Dave and Tony have a solid enough relationship that Tony's skepticism does not deter Dave from speaking the truth in love to Tony. When Tony shares his skepticism of the people from church helping Beth with her preeclampsia, Dave replies, "They do it with a sense of extending grace to anyone who has need of it."

Bad things happen in Tony's life. Beth gets preeclampsia. Christina and Joey are delivered earlier than desired by C-section. Joey's lungs are underdeveloped, and he has to stay in the hospital long after Christina has been released. All of this happens in spite of Dave, Sarah, and Beth's prayers, and it supports Tony's belief that prayer doesn't work because there is no God.

MY STORY

Each person in your group has a story. They have experiences, wants, desires, hardships, longings and secrets. The following questions are designed to help you share your story. Each week you are encouraged to write your responses to the questions in the space provided before you attend your group meeting. This will help you share your thoughts and ideas when your group meets.

Question: Tony resists any help when Beth is confined to bed during her pregnancy. How hard or how easy is it for you to ask for help from others? Why do you think that is?

Question: When have you gone through a particularly difficult time? Did you go through this experience alone or did you have a support team to help you? Who was the most supportive and what was there about them that made them so helpful to you?

BIBLICAL PERSPECTIVE

PRIMING THE PUMP

And they heard the sound of the LORD God walking in the garden in the cool of the day, and the man and his wife hid themselves from the presence of the LORD God among the trees of the garden. But the LORD God called to the man and said to him, "Where are you?"

—GENESIS 3:8–9

Question: In terms of your relationship with God, where are you? Do you feel close to God? Are you distant from God? Are you searching for a relationship with God? Have you walked with God for years?

DIGGING DEEPER

Biblical Principle: <u>Not everyone is ready to hear about God.</u>

And if anyone will not receive you or listen to your words, shake off the dust from your feet when you leave that house or town.

—MATTHEW 10:14

And as He was setting out on His journey, a man ran up and knelt before Him and asked Him, "Good Teacher, what must I do to inherit eternal life?" . . . And Jesus, looking at him, loved him, and said to him, "You lack one thing: go, and sell all that you have and give it to the poor, and you will have treasure in Heaven; and come, follow Me." Disheartened by the saying, he went away sorrowful, for he had great possessions.

—MARK 10:17, 21–22

Question: Dave and Sarah did not hesitate to share spiritual truth with Tony, even though they knew he was not ready to receive it. Why do you think they "got away with" this sharing, not turning Tony off so he would no longer want to be friends with them?

Biblical Principle: <u>God does not shelter us from hardships.</u> <u>God uses hardships in our lives to transform us</u>.

Count it all joy, my brothers, when you meet trials of various kinds, for you know that the testing of your faith produces steadfastness. And let steadfastness have its full effect, that you may be perfect and complete, lacking in nothing.

—JAMES 1:2–4

Not only that, but we rejoice in our sufferings, knowing that suffering produces endurance, and endurance produces character, and character produces hope, and hope does not put us to shame, because God's love has been poured into our hearts through the Holy Spirit who has been given to us.

—ROMANS 5:3–5

Question: When you are going through difficult times, do you believe that in time you will be able to see how God used these difficulties to build character and hope into your life? Can you think of a time in your life when God used difficulties to ultimately bless you?

Question: If you pray for something and you do not get the result you desired, do you think that means that prayer doesn't work? Why or why not?

Biblical Principle: <u>Nothing can separate us from God's love. He promises to never leave us.</u>

For I am sure that neither death nor life, nor angels nor rulers, nor things present nor things to come, nor powers, nor height nor depth, nor anything else in all creation, will be able to separate us from the love of God in Christ Jesus our Lord.

—ROMANS 8:38–39

And behold, I am with you always, to the end of the age.

—MATTHEW 28:20

Question: Tony and Beth experience conflict in their relationship. They work through their conflict and their relationship grows stronger. Have you had a meaningful relationship that experienced conflict and the relationship did not survive? If so, how do you view that experience today? What about a relationship that did survive conflict? What made the difference?

Question: How does it affect you knowing that there is absolutely nothing that you can do, or not do, that would cause God to stop loving you or leave you?

APPLICATION

Information that produces motivation and possibly inspiration, but which does not conclude with application, only leads to frustration.

—Hoyt A. Byrum

But be doers of the Word, and not hearers only, deceiving yourselves. For if anyone is a hearer of the Word and not a doer, he is like a man who looks intently at his natural face in a mirror. For he looks at himself and goes away and at once forgets what he was like. But the one who looks into the perfect law, the law of liberty, and perseveres, being no hearer who forgets but a doer who acts, he will be blessed in his doing.

—James 1:22–25

The purpose of gathering in a small group and discussing biblical principles is not primarily to make you smarter. It is designed to make you different. Therefore, each week you will be asked to apply what you have learned to your life with specific action steps that will help you be "doers of the word."

Action Step: Identify a relationship you have that you would like to improve. Then think of one thing you can implement to further develop that relationship. Establish a time when you will implement this action.

PRAYER LOG

To end each session, each person in the group is invited to share something they are thankful for (joys) and something that they would like prayer for (concerns). They may also wish share how they did on their action step from the previous week. The space below is provided to record these requests so that the group members can pray during the week for each other.

After everyone has shared, you can have an open time of prayer where those who feel comfortable can pray, or one person can offer a closing prayer.

For next week, please read Chapters 13-25 and answer the questions in **SESSION 2**.

THE 3G LIFESTYLE

GRACE, GRATITUDE AND GENEROSITY
CHAPTERS 13-25

We make a living by what we get, but we make a life by what we give.

—WINSTON CHURCHILL

THIS SESSION

Tony is a person who liked to help others—if it wasn't too much of an inconvenience. When Pastor Bob invites him to join some church members on a mission trip, he asks his boss, Jerry, if he can take the time off from his work. Jerry says he can go but that he will have to use his vacation time to make the trip. Tony chooses to go. Pretty big sacrifice and out of character for Tony.

After the trip, Pastor Bob discovers that on the way there, Calvin was influencing Tony to buy into a "works-righteousness" approach to serving others. Calvin clearly is motivated to go on the mission trip so he can have a better chance of getting into Heaven when he dies. But Pastor Bob knows that the Bible teaches us that Heaven is a free gift—a gift of grace (Ephesians 2:8,9). When he discovers that others on the mission trip supported Calvin's point of view, Bob knows he needs to correct this inaccurate perception. Bob leaps into action. He invites them all to a retreat.

On the retreat, Bob not only tries to explain clearly that salvation is a gift of God (Grace) but that when we grasp the significance of God's Grace, we naturally are filled with Gratitude. And once we live our lives out of a paradigm of gratitude (the opposite of entitlement) we find our joy in life from being Generous. There it is: The 3G Lifestyle.

Every experience in life can be a sign of God's grace, even the difficult experiences. You can find reasons to thank God for them. *Give thanks in all circumstances, for this is the will of God in Christ Jesus for you* (1 Thessalonians 5:18). And you can share the meaning behind every life experience with others in a spirit of generosity.

Life is best lived when we simplify it. When we unclutter it. When we remove complexity from it. Embracing the belief that the whole of the Christian life can be understood in light of God's Grace, our Gratitude, and expressing Generosity is practical and biblical at the same time. Enjoy discussing this with your fellow group members.

MY STORY

On the way to the mission trip, Calvin explains to Tony how helping others helps you get into Heaven. Pastor Bob says Heaven is a free gift (Grace) to those who ask Jesus Christ to come into their lives.

Question: Do you think more like Calvin or Pastor Bob? Why?

Question: Who in your life has been the most loving, grace-centered, generous person? How have they demonstrated that to you?

Question: When did you last make a significant sacrifice to help someone in need? Was it a sacrifice of time? Of money? Of convenience? Why did you choose to help?

BIBLICAL PERSPECTIVE

PRIMING THE PUMP

The definition of Grace is *unmerited divine assistance given to humans for their regeneration or sanctification; a virtue coming from God,* according to the Merriam-Webster Dictionary.

Question: How would you define Grace?

DIGGING DEEPER

Biblical Principle: <u>Our good works do not save us. Jesus'</u>
<u>good work (dying on a cross) saves us.</u>

For by grace you have been saved through faith. And this is not your own doing; it is the gift of God, not a result of works, so that no one may boast.

—EPHESIANS 2:8–9

For if, because of one man's trespass, death reigned through that one man, much more will those who receive the abundance of grace and the free gift of righteousness reign in life through the one man, Jesus Christ. Therefore, as one trespass led to condemnation for all men, so one act of righteousness leads to justification and life for all men.

—ROMANS 5:17–18

Question: Dr. Callahan explains his view of faith and belief to Tony in Chapter 18 of *The Chase*. If the Bible says we are saved by God's grace and our faith, what does it mean to you to have faith? How do you demonstrate your faith?

Question: How hard or how easy is it (or was it) for you to stop trying to earn your way into Heaven? Have you actually stopped?

Biblical Principle: Gratitude is the natural result of accepting God's freely given Grace.

On the way to Jerusalem, He was passing along between Samaria and Galilee. And as He entered a village, He was met by ten lepers, who stood at a distance and lifted up their voices, saying, "Jesus, Master, have mercy on us." When He saw them He said to them, "Go and show yourselves to the priests." And as they went they were cleansed. Then one of them, when he saw that he was healed, turned back, praising God with a loud voice; and he fell on his face at Jesus' feet, giving Him thanks. Now he was a Samaritan. Then Jesus answered, "Were not ten cleansed? Where are the nine? Was no one found to return and give praise to God except this foreigner?" And He said to him, "Rise and go your way; your faith has made you well.

—LUKE 17:11–19

Question: Ten lepers received God's grace and were healed, but only one came back and thanked Jesus. Why do you think the others did not express their gratitude? Could they have not recognized their healing as grace from God? How could that be?

Biblical Principle: Being Grateful for the free gift of Grace leads us to be Generous with our time, talents and resources.

And behold, a woman of the city, who was a sinner, when she learned that He was reclining at table in the Pharisee's house, brought an alabaster flask of ointment, and standing behind Him at His feet, weeping, she began to wet His feet with her tears and wiped them with the hair of her head and kissed His feet and anointed them with the ointment.

—LUKE 7:38–39

Now the full number of those who believed were of one heart and soul, and no one said that any of the things that belonged to him was his own, but they had everything in common. And with great power the apostles were giving their testimony to the resurrection of the Lord Jesus, and great grace was upon them all. There was not a needy person among them, for as many as were owners of lands or houses sold them and brought the proceeds of what was sold and laid it at the apostles' feet, and it was distributed to each as any had need.

—ACTS 4:32–35

Question: Scholars tell us that the oil in the alabaster flask was worth about a year's income. What do you think prompted her to be so extravagant in showing her love for Jesus?

Question: Throughout the Book of Acts, the early church is portrayed as being generous. The early followers of Christ shared their individual abundance with those who were in need (Acts 4:32-47). What would it be like to live in such a community? Is the local church you may be part of, living with the spirit of generosity? If so, how?

Biblical Principle: Prayer is one of the primary ways we experience intimacy with God. It is not primarily a way to get what we want from God.

Then He said to them, "My soul is very sorrowful, even to death; remain here, and watch with Me." And going a little farther He fell on His face and prayed, saying, "My Father, if it be possible, let this cup pass from Me; nevertheless, not as I will, but as You will.

—MATTHEW 26:38–39

Be gracious to me, O Lord! See my affliction from those who hate me, O You who lift me up from the gates of death, that I may recount all Your praises, that in the gates of the daughter of Zion I may rejoice in your salvation.

—PSALM 9:13–14

Question: The scriptures frequently speak of Jesus rising early in the morning, going out to a lonely place, and praying to His Father in Heaven (Mark 1:35). What can you learn from Jesus' prayer in Gethsemane (Matthew 26:38-39) about requests and expectations?

Question: Is your prayer life more like David who poured out his heart to God for the purpose of intimacy with God (Psalm 51) or is your prayer life more like those who write letters to Santa in November so they can be blessed on Christmas morning? Explain.

APPLICATION

Information that produces motivation and possibly inspiration, but which does not conclude with application, only leads to frustration.

—HOYT A. BYRUM

For the Lord will not forsake His people, for His great name's sake, because it has pleased the Lord to make you a people for Himself. Moreover, as for me, far be it from me that I should sin against the Lord by ceasing to pray for you, and I will instruct you in the good and the right way. Only fear the Lord and serve Him faithfully with all your heart. For consider what great things He has done for you.

—1 SAMUEL 12: 22–24

Action Step: Samuel told the people of God to remember the great things that God had done for them (1 Samuel 12:24). Your action step for this week is to consider all of the blessings that God has given you over the years. List some of the most significant blessings in the space below.

PRAYER LOG

For next week, please read Chapters 27-31 and
answer the questions in **SESSION 3**.

PEACE WITH GOD: PART 1

THE THREE-LEGGED STOOL
CHAPTERS 27–31

Nothing, absolutely nothing befalls those who 'love God and are called according to His purpose' but what is for our deepest and highest good. Therefore, the mercy and the sovereignty of God are the twin pillars of my life.

—JOHN PIPER, *Desiring God:Meditations of a Christian Hedonist*

THIS SESSION

Where does stability in life come from? It can't come from circumstances because they change so quickly and so disruptively. So where can we find what we need to have a solid foundation that won't be shaken by a disturbing medical report? By an unfaithful spouse? By a teen who isn't running with a wholesome crowd? By a company that chooses to relocate and can't take everyone with them—like you?

In *The Chase*, Pastor Bob says that true stability in life occurs when you put your weight on a three-legged stool. A one-legged stool doesn't have a chance of giving you safety and security. Two legged stools can hold you for a while, but just shift your weight a little, and you and the stool will easily topple.

Pastor Bob says that there is a three-legged stool that is totally capable of letting you sit upon it or stand upon it and it will hold you. It is strong enough to support you no matter what. These legs are: making God's Word authoritative in your life; basing your Assurance of Salvation on God's Word, not your feelings; and acknowledging Jesus as the Lord and Boss of your life, taking yourself off the throne and bending your knee to Jesus.

Imagine for a moment having a blueprint for your life that is designed by the Almighty Creator of the Universe who loves you. Imagine never having to worry if you are good enough to enter into God's presence and Jesus' arms when this life is over. Imagine having the Person who loves you the most in all of the universe and who has resources at His command that are more sufficient than you will ever need leading your life in a perfect way. Sounds pretty safe and secure, doesn't it? It is far more than that. It provides a great adventure today and it will lead to a "Party of all Parties" when this life is concluded.

The rest of the teachings from *The Chase* are important. But if all three of the legs just mentioned are not in place in your life, the other key elements of the Christian life won't be sufficient to keep you at peace. Pretty important stuff, wouldn't you say?

MY STORY

Let's start with leg one: the authority of God's Word. Every Sunday preachers stand in the pulpit and "proclaim" the Word of God. So what? Not everyone listening has come to the place where they can say, "Pastor, if that's what the Word of God says, then I am committed to believing it and doing it."

Tony says he doesn't care if the Bible said God owned everything, even his house. He isn't buying it. "Pick and choose" is the most common practice of churchgoers. They take what they like from God's Word and discard or ignore the rest.

Question: So, what is the Bible for you? Is it simply a history book that tells you what happened long ago or is it a book that gives you the answers and direction for your life in the 21st century? Explain.

The second leg of the stool is living with the assurance of your salvation. Assurance is based upon what God says in the Bible and not your feelings. Living without assurance of salvation can cause great uncertainty and anxiety.

Question: If you died tonight, do you think you would be in Heaven with God? Most people answer, "I hope so." What would you say? If God asked you, "Why should I let you into Heaven?" what would you say?*

The third leg of the stool is about who is in control of your life. Calvin liked helping in the bike ministry at the Bread of Life soup kitchen because he could maintain control. He could decide how many bikes he would repair and when he would work on them.

Like Calvin, Pastor Bob didn't want to give up control of his life to God because he thought he already had a pretty good plan for his life and it was working just fine. Bob's problem was he believed that if God was in charge of his life, God would make his life miserable.

---

* *Evangelism Explosion,* by D. James Kennedy

Question: In what ways does letting God take control of your life appeal to you? In what ways does it scare you?

BIBLICAL PERSPECTIVE

PRIMING THE PUMP

In the United States, we have a representative form of government. That means that we vote for individuals to represent us and make laws and regulations on our behalf. This includes the President on down the chain of command. When we have issues with those laws, we take them to court, sometimes up to the Supreme Court. When the court makes a decision, we live by the decision handed down.

Question: What gives the government the right and authority to dictate how we live and how we interact with our fellow citizens? What gives God the authority to direct us regarding how we should live?

DIGGING DEEPER

Biblical Principle: <u>God's Word is reliable and trustworthy.</u>
<u>Thus, it is authoritative.</u>

*In the beginning, God created the Heavens and the earth. The earth
was without form and void, and darkness was over the face of the deep.
And the Spirit of God was hovering over the face of the waters. And
God said, "Let there be light." And there was light. And God saw that
the light was good.*

—**GENESIS 1:1–3**

*All Scripture is breathed out by God and profitable for teaching, for
reproof, for correction, and for training in righteousness, that the man
of God may be complete, equipped for every good work.*

—**2 TIMOTHY 3:16–17**

Question: Given the Bible is God's "playbook" for teaching you,
correcting you, and training you in righteous living, do you use it
that way? Do you go to the Bible when you need guidance and
direction? If not, why not? Can you think of an example of when
the Bible gave you specific guidance for making a decision?

Biblical Principle: Having assurance of your salvation lets you live with the peace that you don't' have to earn your way into Heaven.

My sheep hear My voice, and I know them, and they follow Me. I give them eternal life, and they will never perish, and no one will snatch them out of My hand. My Father, who has given them to Me, is greater than all, and no one is able to snatch them out of the Father's hand. I and the Father are one.

—JOHN 10:27–30

In Him, you also, when you heard the word of truth, the gospel of your salvation, and believed in Him, were sealed with the promised Holy Spirit, who is the guarantee of our inheritance until we acquire possession of it, to the praise of His glory.

—EPHESIANS 1:13–14

Question: If we accept the authority of the Bible and the Bible says that those who have received Jesus into their lives have salvation, what does that mean to you? Are you worried about what happens when you die? How else do you live differently than those who do not accept the Bible as being relevant to their lives today?

Biblical Principle: <u>Jesus is the Lord of the universe. But you must acknowledge Him as Lord of your life and live with Him as your Boss.</u>

For I know the plans I have for you, declares the Lord, plans for welfare and not for evil, to give you a future and a hope.

—JEREMIAH 29:11

And Simon answered, "Master, we toiled all night and took nothing! But at Your word I will let down the nets."

—LUKE 5:5

Pastor Bob resisted living with Jesus as his Lord and Boss. Why? Because he believed that the plan he had for his life was superior to whatever plan God might have. Living with Jesus as your Lord is an essential leg in the three-legged stool.

Question: What are some reasons you can think of why a person would not want to make Jesus the Lord and Boss of their life? What are some reasons you can think of why a person *would* want to make Jesus the Lord and Boss of their life?

Peter was a fisherman; Jesus was a carpenter (or a mason working with stone). Peter had worked his nets all night and caught nothing. Peter was tired. There are probably fifty other reasons why Peter could have responded to Jesus' words with something like, "Jesus, I'm going home. I'm beat." But he didn't. He responded to Jesus as we are to respond to Jesus: "But at Your word, I will."

Question: What would it take for you to become a "But at Your word, I will" Christian?

APPLICATION

Information that produces motivation and possibly inspiration, but which does not conclude with application, only leads to frustration.

—HOYT A. BYRUM

Action Step: Identify one area of your life that you have not given up to God's control. Why is surrendering to God on this issue so difficult for you? Describe what you will do to let go and trust God with this issue.

PRAYER LOG

For next week, read Chapters 32-37 and
answer the questions in **SESSION 4**.

PEACE WITH GOD: PART 2

OUR VALUES AND OUR VALUABLES
CHAPTERS 32–37

Embedded in our fallen human nature is a clash between two value systems: the temporal and the eternal. Our natural disposition is to look to and be shaped by temporal things as if they were eternal. But that value system never really delivers what it promises. It leads to emptiness, delusion, and foolishness. It's only when we take the risk of embracing the eternal value system over the temporal that we find true fulfillment, reality, and wisdom.

—KEN BOA, **President of Reflections Ministries**

THIS SESSION

In this session, we will look at aligning our value system with God's. And we will look at the whole issue of ownership verses stewardship. The last thing in our lives to relinquish to God's control is usually our wallet or purse. Letting go of one's "purse strings" is a struggle for most, unless you have completely embraced the belief that God's plan for your life is one that will bless you and you have nothing to worry about.

Remember, we are to make God's Word authoritative in our lives. We are to become like Peter. *Master, we toiled all night and caught nothing. But at Your word, I will let down the nets.* (Luke 5:5). Peter never experienced abundance like he did that day when he let go of his own wisdom and skill and will.

We are to acknowledge Jesus as the Boss, the one who directs our lives. When it comes to our values and our valuables, we are talking about what is dear to us. We work hard to accumulate our wealth and we believe our safety and security is directly related to what we have "in the vault." Can we really trust our finances to him? Can we really live with the intention of blessing others first and living on what remains?

Dave and Sarah were givers. They gave God their tithe (10 percent of their income) every month and trusted him to meet their needs. Dr. Callahan was a giver. He believed that those who had significant resources needed to give at what he called a "significant level" that might challenge them to give beyond the tithe—maybe 13 or 14 percent. The members of the church were givers. They gave of themselves, in terms of their time, to Tony and Beth sacrificially when Tony and Beth were in need due to Beth's preeclampsia. Time, talent, and resources all have significant value. People who invest those resources generously in people have found the way to experience significance and joy in their lives.

So let's tackle the whole issue of values (what matters most) and valuables (time, talent, resources). But just know, the Bible says you can't serve both God and mammon (a biblical term for riches, or wealth, or money) in Matthew 6:24. Did I hear someone say "Ouch"?

We should note that values are self-determined. We decide what ours are, based on our experiences, situation, and relationships.

MY STORY

Pastor Bob says that having an eternal value system means that God's Word and people matter to you more than worldly things. Why? Because people and God's Word will live eternally. Living with a temporal value system means that things of this world (that which you have now but can't take with you when you die) matter most.

Question: How can you know what your value system is? Some say just look in your checkbook. What evidence does it contain that you are investing in people (church, para-church ministries, soup kitchens, homeless ministries, people in general) and what evidence does your calendar contain that you are investing your time in personal devotions, serving your church, and generally helping others in need?

Question: Ken Boa (see quote above) says that a temporal value system leads to emptiness, delusion, and foolishness. He says the eternal value system leads to fulfillment, reality, and wisdom. What do you think?

BIBLICAL PERSPECTIVE

PRIMING THE PUMP

Not that I am speaking of being in need, for I have learned in whatever situation I am to be content. I know how to be brought low, and I know how to abound. In any and every circumstance, I have learned the secret of facing plenty and hunger, abundance and need. I can do all things through Him who strengthens me.

—PHILIPPIANS 4:11–13

Question: Twice in Philippians 4:11–13, Paul said he learned to be content. That means it didn't come naturally. Paul states that contentment is not defined by circumstances. Living with abundance or scarcity did not influence his state of contentment. In what ways are you content? In what ways are you discontent?

DIGGING DEEPER

Biblical Principle: God values people.

And they were bringing children to Him that He might touch them, and the disciples rebuked them. But when Jesus saw it, He was indignant and said to them, "Let the children come to Me; do not hinder them, for to such belongs the kingdom of God."

—MARK 10:13–14

A woman from Samaria came to draw water. Jesus said to her, "Give Me a drink." (For His disciples had gone away into the city to buy food.) The Samaritan woman said to Him, "How is it that You, a Jew, ask for a drink from me, a woman of Samaria?" (For Jews have no dealings with Samaritans.) Jesus answered her, "If you knew the gift of God, and Who it is that is saying to you, 'Give Me a drink,' you would have asked Him, and He would have given you living water."

—JOHN 4:7–10

In Chapter 33 of *The Chase*, Calvin asks Tony to help with the Bread of Life bike ministry. Tony declines, in part because he sees the homeless as not worthy of his time. However, no one is unimportant to Jesus. Everyone matters. Any and all can come to Jesus, and He would not turn them away. Why? Because people have eternal value. Everything on earth will one day decay, or rust, or cease to work. Their bodies will die, but their souls will live forever.

Question: Who are the people in your life that you value most? Why?

Jesus invested Himself in people who were outcasts. For the Jews, no group of people were more offensive than the Samaritans. In the story above, John tells us that Jesus is going from Judea to Galilee. The text says that Jesus "had to pass through Samaria (John 4:4)." Jews did not "pass through Samaria" to get to Galilee. They walked around Samaria, making the trip much longer. Why did Jesus "have" to go through Samaria? Because He knew that God's plan for Him was to invest time in the life of a Samaritan woman who was an outcast among the Jews as well as her own people. That encounter changed her life.

In our world today, divisions among people are rampant. Jesus does not see color, race, or status. Jesus sees eternal souls, each having significant value. He does not move away from people; He moves towards them.

Question: How can we become more like Jesus, seeing all people as being worthy of love and support? Why is it so hard for us to live this way?

Biblical Principle: The Bible is clear: we are not supposed to store up treasures on earth (temporal value system). We are to "lay up for yourself treasures in Heaven" (eternal value system).

Do not lay up for yourselves treasures on earth, where moth and rust destroy and where thieves break in and steal, but lay up for yourselves treasures in Heaven, where neither moth nor rust destroy and where thieves do not break in and steal. For where your treasure is, there your heart will be also.

—MATTHEW 6:19–21

Question: Do you think these verses mean you should not have a savings account for "a rainy day"? That you should not have a retirement account for when you cease to be employed? What do these verses in Matthew mean to you?

Question: The Bible says where you put your treasure, that's where your heart will be also (Matthew 6:21). That means, if you don't currently have a heart for eternal things (people and God's Word), start investing in them now (with your time, talent, and resources) and your heart will go there. That's what happened in Tony's life. He started tithing, even before he was a Christian, and his heart was drawn to eternal matters over time. Do you think if you took more of your time, talent, and resources and invested them into eternal things it would change your heart? How?

Biblical Principle: <u>God is the owner of everything on earth. We are the stewards, or caregivers, or trustees of God's resources.</u>

The earth is the Lord's and the fullness thereof, the world and those who dwell therein, for He has founded it upon the seas and established it upon the rivers.

—PSALM 24:1–2

Beware lest you say in your heart, "My power and the might of my hand have gotten me this wealth." You shall remember the Lord your God, for it is He who gives you power to get wealth, that He may confirm His covenant that He swore to your fathers, as it is this day.

—DEUTERONOMY 8:17–18

Question: Trustees manage someone else's financial resources. They manage them according to the owner's wishes. What do you think are God's wishes regarding the way you are presently managing His resources?

Question: It is natural to think as Tony did, "I have earned this money. It's mine. I can do what I want with it." What would it take for a person who thinks this way to embrace the biblical perspective, that God is the One Who owns it all and He is the One Who gave you the skills, training, and opportunity to earn what you earn?

Bibical Principle: <u>Demonstrating generosity to others is</u> <u>evidence that we understand grace and have gratitude for</u> <u>all God gives us.</u>

The idea that all we have is God's, not ours, is probably the most difficult biblical teaching presented in *The Chase*. But the authors of *The Chase* have not refrained from including it. Why? Because for those who have determined, "If God said it, I believe it and I will do it," the concept of being a steward of God's earthly treasures is the key to developing a lifestyle of generosity. Here is the logic.

1. If everything we have belongs to God, we had better take good care of it.
2. If God trusts me to take care of His treasures, He will let me know when He wants me to pass those treasures onto someone else.
3. God has already instructed us to demonstrate that we honor Him as God by returning the tithe (the first fruits) to Kingdom work.

Question: In *The Chase*, Dr. Callahan believed that the amount of money you invest in Kingdom work should be significant for you. The amount of money that is significant for you may be greater or lesser than others. Significant giving is giving that causes you to make sacrifices. For some, 2 percent of your income can be significant. For others, significance might be 14 percent or more of their income. What are your thoughts on Dr. Callahan's perspective?

Question: Christians often think that if they start tithing then they are free to do as they please with the remaining 90 percent. But God owns 100 percent of our resources. As trustees of God's resources, we are accountable to Him for how we manage all of our (His) money. Would God have you manage the money you use for your own needs differently than the way you currently manage it? How?

APPLICATION

Information that produces motivation and possibly inspiration, but which does not conclude with application, only leads to frustration.

—HOYT A. BYRUM

We have covered a large number of very challenging topics in this session: people are valued by God; God is the owner of all that we have; we are to manage 100 percent of our resources according to His will; and we are to be generous out of a deep sense of gratitude.

Most of us have not arrived at the place where God wants us to be on all these issues.

Action Step: Identify where you think God wants you to focus your energies concerning one of these issues. What, specifically, does He want you to change?

PRAYER LOG

For next week, please read Chapters 38-42 and
answer the questions in **SESSION 5**.

CONNECTIONS AND COMMUNITY

COMMUNITY IS A BLESSING
CHAPTERS 38–42

Let God have you, and let God love you—and don't be surprised if your heart begins to hear music you've never heard and your feet learn to dance as never before.

—MAX LUCADO, **best-selling Christian author**

THIS SESSION

In this session we will look at how community is part of God's plan for our lives. Without community and the ability to connect with each other and with God, God's plan for the world would be much more difficult to realize.

Tony believes that he does not need to be part of a community. He is capable of living his life pretty much on his own, with the exception of having Beth, Dave, and Sarah in his life. Even when he finds himself facing a difficult time with Beth's medical condition which will require her to have bed-rest for months, he initially puts on his "Superman cape" and says, "I can handle it."

Tony is also a private person. He wants nothing to do with having people he doesn't even know coming into his home and caring for Beth. "Who are these people?" he asks. "Why would they want to help us? What do they want from us in return for helping?" Because Tony does not yet have a grateful spirit nor a generous heart, he cannot understand those who do.

It is often in Christian community that we experience God's grace. God extends His grace to us through people. He extended His grace for our salvation through Jesus. He extends His grace to us through those who give to us without any expectation of "return or payment."

Because Tony is not a person who likes to receive help, he figures others are like him. Let them put on their own "Superman capes" and get their lives in order on their own, just like he is doing. So it is not surprising that Tony initially turns Calvin down when asked to fix a bicycle for the Bread of Life soup kitchen clientele. He doesn't think very highly of those who are homeless, and he isn't motivated to help. Besides, he is too busy with demands from work and trying to keep up with the responsibilities he has now that he is a father.

But God is at work in Tony's life. Tony agrees to join Calvin for a meeting with Mr. Rodriguez at the soup kitchen and he finds out that Jonathan is the one who will receive the bicycle Calvin gave him to fix. Tony decides to fix the bicycle and weeks later has a surprising conversation with Jonathan. Tony is out of his comfort zone when he hangs out with the Bread of Life clientele but his conversation with Jonathan powerfully begins the process of Tony's "heart transplant." Tony is now experiencing community in an entirely different way.

And when George shows up at Tony's house, Tony listens and learns that he can have a positive impact on George. But it only works because Tony finally took the time to truly listen. And that only happened because Tony and George were part of a small group of men who spent time together, who were in community. God speaks to us through those in our community.

Tony also receives messages from God in unique ways: Beth's insistence on having children, the five-dollar bill, and Dave's dream.

MY STORY

We have said that the Christian life is all about community. The Bible says that the Christian community is like a body. Some are hands, some are eyes, and some are feet. The body of Christ is only healthy when we are connected to and respect one another (1 Corinthians 12:12-31).

Question: When have you been the one who came alongside another person and made a difference in their lives when they had a significant need? How did you help?

Question: George's faith was tested when Jason, the young man he was mentoring, died. Has your faith been tested? If so, how? How did you respond? Was there someone who helped you through that process?

BIBLICAL PERSPECTIVE

PRIMING THE PUMP

We see many instances in the Old Testament where God speaks verbally to many leaders and prophets. God spoke verbally to Moses and gave him the Ten Commandments (Exodus 20). God spoke verbally to Joshua and told him how to bring down the walls of Jericho (Joshua: 6). God spoke verbally to Samuel and told him to admonish the people of Israel (1 Samuel 8:9).

Question: As far as we know, we do not hear of such verbal communications between God and people today. Why do you think this is?

For the body does not consist of one member but of many. If the foot should say, "Because I am not a hand, I do not belong to the body," that would not make it any less a part of the body. And if the ear should say, "Because I am not an eye, I do not belong to the body," that would not make it any less a part of the body. If the whole body were an eye, where would be the sense of hearing? If the whole body were an ear, where would be the sense of smell? But as it is, God arranged the members in the body, each one of them, as He chose. If all were a single member, where would the body be? As it is, there are many parts,[e] yet one body. The eye cannot say to the hand, "I have no need of you," nor again the head to the feet, "I have no need of you."

—1 CORINTHIANS 12:14–21

Question: Paul is telling us in Corinthians that we cannot live apart from our fellow Christians. Community is essential for us to survive. How have you reached out to expand and enhance your community?

DIGGING DEEPER

Biblical Principle: <u>God communicates with us in ways that we are not often expecting.</u>

The next day, as they were on their journey and approaching the city, Peter went up on the housetop about the sixth hour to pray. And he became hungry and wanted something to eat, but while they were preparing it, he fell into a trance and saw the Heavens opened and something like a great sheet descending, being let down by its four corners upon the earth. In it were all kinds of animals and reptiles and birds of the air. And there came a voice to him: "Rise, Peter, kill and eat." But Peter said, "By no means, Lord; for I have never eaten anything that is common or unclean." And the voice came to him again a second time, "What God has made clean, do not call common."

—ACTS 10:9–15

Peter receives a message from God through a vision, and a voice from Heaven (Acts 10:9-17). Tony receives several messages from God. He gets the five-dollar bill with a scripture reference on it and saves it. Dave tells him of his dream about a big fight with his father. God was chasing after Tony.

Question: Have you ever received a message from God that you didn't recognize as such until later? What was the message and how did God reveal it to you?

Biblical Principle: God's love for us and acceptance of us motivates us to love others.

When they had finished breakfast, Jesus said to Simon Peter, "Simon, son of John, do you love Me more than these?" He said to Him, "Yes, Lord; You know that I love You." He said to him, "Feed My lambs."

—JOHN 21:15

Peter had denied Christ and he returned to being a fisherman (Matthew 26:69-75). Jesus later met Peter on the shore and restored him to his calling: spreading the Gospel, and being a fisher of men. In that moment of restoration, Jesus addressed the issue of motivation. In John 21, Jesus tells Peter that He wants him to give his life away to others with the motivation being his love for Christ.

When Tony met with Jonathan, he was blown away at Jonathan's story. He realized that his own efforts to repair a bicycle for Jonathan had a dramatic impact on Jonathan's life.

Question: When did you put yourself out to help someone else? Was it helping at your child's school? Was it helping someone at your place of work complete a task? What motivated you to do that? How did that make you feel? Did you see Jesus smiling as you gave yourself generously to someone who matters to God?

Biblical Principle: <u>Loving our neighbors matters to God.</u>

But he, desiring to justify himself, said to Jesus, "And who is my neighbor?"

—LUKE 10:29

Jesus tells the story of the Good Samaritan. In the story, a man is lying almost dead on the side of the road. A priest and a Levite see the man and pass him by. However, a Samaritan (hated by the Jews) stops, takes care of the man, and covers the expenses needed to see that the man recovers. Jesus says the Samaritan is the neighbor (Luke 10:25-37).

Question: How would Jesus define who your neighbor is today?

Question: Have you had a time when you were aware that God had positioned you in a certain place and a certain time to give your time, talent, or resources to another and it was not planned by you? Did you respond like the priest and the Levite (who walked on by) or like the Good Samaritan (who stopped and helped)?

But Moses said to the Lord, "Oh, my Lord, I am not eloquent, either in the past or since You have spoken to Your servant, but I am slow of speech and of tongue." Then the Lord said to him, "Who has made man's mouth? Who makes him mute, or deaf, or seeing, or blind? Is it not I, the Lord? Now therefore go, and I will be with your mouth and teach you what you shall speak."

—EXODUS 4:10–12

Question: God sends Moses to do a job that Moses feels ill-prepared to do (Exodus Chapters 3 and 4). God says "go." George comes to Tony in a moment of crisis. Tony does not feel prepared to help George, especially regarding George's faith. Yet he is able to help George because God speaks through Tony to give George comfort. Describe a time when you were "positioned" to help someone, and you weren't sure you could do it—but you tried. How did it go?

APPLICATION

Information that produces motivation and possibly inspiration, but which does not conclude with application, only leads to frustration.

—HOYT A. BYRUM

God often places us in situations that we are not prepared for. Yet the Bible tells us that God always equips us with what we need.

Action Step: In the next few weeks, look for someone whom God places in your life who has issues that you would not normally be able or willing to address. See if you can trust God to help you help that person.

PRAYER LOG

For next week, read Chapters 43-48 and
answer the questions in **SESSION 6**.

SESSION 6

CATCHING GOD

NOT THE END, BUT THE BEGINNING
CHAPTERS 43–48

Religion says do. Jesus says done. Religion is man searching for God. Jesus is God searching for man. Religion is pursuing God by our moral efforts. Jesus is God pursuing us despite our moral efforts. Religious people kill for what they believe. Jesus' followers die for what they believe.

—JEFFERSON BETHKE, Christian author

THIS SESSION

We have seen Tony experience events he never expected to have and people he never expected to meet. But all these things are overshadowed by the sudden and unexpected death of his father. Many of us have had such experiences and we all have our own ways to process them. The events that follow in *The Chase* show how God can take terrible situations that He did not cause and use them for His own purposes.

You may not buy into that thought. The idea that God uses bad things for good seems to many to be a cop-out. But the reality is that Jesus never promised us a rose garden. Life for all of us can be hard, and it can be cruel. The fact that we believe in God and have accepted Jesus into our hearts will not ensure that we will avoid hardships, disappointments, and tragedies. However, it is the way in which we respond to those events that makes the difference.

At the conclusion of the book Tony takes an action step. After meeting with Pastor Bob, he begins to jog home to pray with his wife, Beth. He is taking the first step in his journey to "catch God." He is about to experience his "second birth."

You may have taken that step years ago. You may have never taken that step. No one can take that step for you. We will conclude this session by encouraging you to take your next step. What will it be? Like Tony, your next step may be to pray to receive Jesus Christ into your heart. It might be to settle the issue regarding who will be the CEO of your life—acknowledging Jesus as the Lord and Boss of your life. It may be a commitment to let God direct your financial life and start investing more in Kingdom work and less in "treasures on earth."

MY STORY

This session is about listening to God, being honest with yourself, and acting in faith as the Spirit of God whispers to you. Choose now to be responsive to what you are being led to do.

Tony knows that running is nothing more than taking one step at a time at a pace your body allows. So it is with the Christian life. It involves taking one step at a time at a pace your spirit allows. Join the race. Finish strong. Celebrate the prize that awaits you at the finish line. But know that whatever step you take next, it is merely the beginning of the rest of your journey, not the end.

Question: After Tony's father dies, Tony is running and finds himself in front of Pastor Bob's house. Did God lead him there or was it a coincidence? Why do you say that?

Question: Tony pleads with God to save his father, even though Tony doesn't yet believe in God. Do you think God answers the pleas of those who don't believe in Him? Why or why not?

Question: George calls Tony right after Tony hears about his father's death. George doesn't even know why he called, but he knew he "had to call." This is an example of a connected community. With whom do you have such a close connection that they "just know" when you need them?

BIBLICAL PERSPECTIVE

PRIMING THE PUMP

I have told you these things, so that in Me you may have peace. In this world you will have trouble. But take heart! I have overcome the world.

—JOHN 16:33

Question: Many Christians get angry with God when they experience hardships and disappointments, thinking that God should have protected them from such difficulties (Lamentations 3). Why do you think people have that expectation when it is clear that followers of Christ suffer just like anyone else?

DIGGING DEEPER

Biblical Principle: God is not absent when we experience adversity. He is preparing to use the adversity to draw us closer to Himself.

Count it all joy, my brothers, when you meet trials of various kinds, for you know that the testing of your faith produces steadfastness. And let steadfastness have its full effect, that you may be perfect and complete, lacking nothing.

—JAMES 1:2–5

Question: The Apostle James makes a bold claim when he says it is through trials that we are perfected. Trials test our faith. Trials are good for building our faith. Faith is good for enduring trials. So, describe a time when you experienced a "trial" and you failed miserably, got angry, and asked God, "Why me?" Describe a time when you "passed the test" and believed that God was present in the trial and that He would produce something good out of it.

Biblical Principle: There are no coincidences or mistakes with God, only evidences that God is working His plan for our lives.

As for you, you meant evil against me, but God meant it for good, to bring it about that many people should be kept alive, as they are today. So do not fear, I will provide for you and your little ones.

—GENESIS 50:20

And we know that for those who love God all things work together for good, for those who are called according to His purpose.

—ROMANS 8:28

One of the great stories in the Old Testament is the story of Joseph in Genesis 50. His brothers sell him into slavery. In Egypt, he spends years in prison, but God ultimately elevates him to second in command to the Pharaoh. When Israel experiences a famine, his family comes to Egypt and Joseph shows grace and mercy to them, meeting their need for food and shelter.

Question: How helpful would it be for you to approach every difficulty, trial, or hardship with the belief that God can use this for good? Have you experienced this before in your life? Explain.

Question: One of the things that had a significant impact upon Tony was when he connected the dots regarding "coincidences." When he thought about the five-dollar bill with Scripture on it (Saul's blindness and conversion), Dave's dream (Tom's death), the same Scripture at his father's funeral and the next day's worship service (Luke 24:13–35—Jesus on the Road to Emmaus), he concluded, "Just too many coincidences. I can't do anything but believe that there is a God behind all of this."

Have there been things in your life that you believed were just coincidences at the time, but might have been "nudgings" from God to draw you nearer to Him? If so, what do you think God was trying to tell you?

Biblical Principle: <u>God is the one pursuing us. He initiates a</u> <u>relationship with us.</u>

You did not choose Me but I chose you and appointed you that you should go and bear fruit and that your fruit should abide, so that whatever you ask the Father in My name, He may give it to you.

—JOHN 15:16

Blessed be the God and Father of our Lord Jesus Christ, Who has blessed us in Christ with every spiritual blessing in the Heavenly places, even as He chose us in Him before the foundation of the world . . . In love He predestined us for adoption to Himself as sons through Jesus Christ, according to the purpose of His will, to the praise of His glorious grace . . .

—EPHESIANS 1:1–6

Behold, I stand at the door and knock. If anyone hears My voice and opens the door, I will come in to him and eat with him, and he with Me.

—REVELATION 3:20

God says we don't choose Him—He chooses us.

God says He adopts us into His family.

God says He knocks on the door of our hearts and asks us to open the door and let Him in.

Question: Do you believe that God has been chasing you? What evidence do you have of that? Have you turned and caught Him? Why or why not?

APPLICATION

Where to begin? All races start at the starting line. Some races are longer than others: 5K, half marathon, full marathon. But they all start at the same place.

The first step in the "Christian Race" is making the decision to open the door of your heart and invite Jesus in to have fellowship with you.

Pastor Bob explained it this way.

Plan: God has a plan for your life—a plan to have a relationship with you.

Problem: The problem is your sin. Sin separates us from God. The penalty for your sin is death.

Provision: Jesus died on the cross to pay the penalty for your sin.

Decision: Jesus pursues you—knocks on the door to your heart. Only you can decide to say "yes" to God, open the door to your heart, and invite Jesus in.

We have concluded each session with an action step. So often, we attend study sessions and while we may learn something new, we often do not make the life changes that we learned about. This is because we go back into the real world and use the same old techniques for dealing with our issues. These techniques have become comfortable for us and changing them is frightening and difficult. Therefore, we are suggesting that, if you are ready to break this cycle, this can only be done over time and with effort. Change is not an instant event, it's a process. So, here is what we are asking you to do:

ACTION STEPS:

1. Understanding the three G's of The 3G Lifestyle is not intuitive. It requires some thought and study. It requires reflection. The best way to learn something is to teach it. So, we recommend that you take some time to review the lessons in this study guide and perhaps do some additional study on your own. Then, when you are ready, find someone who was not in the group with you and explain what you have learned to them. If, as a result of your teaching, they come to understand these concepts, you will truly understand the material better yourself.

2. Once you have this new understanding firmly implanted in your mind, you will naturally see the changes you need to make in your life to follow The 3G Lifestyle. They may be subtle changes, or they may be major ones. Likely there will be both. But don't try to make these changes all at once. That will almost certainly fail. Once you have identified what you intend to do, think about how and when you will make these changes. Develop a plan for your life-change, complete with a timeline and checkpoints. In this way, you can take a measured approach that will allow you to make these changes permanent. Establish a deadline for when you will have a first draft of your plan complete. We say *draft* because your plan will likely change over time.

3. Finally, you probably can't do all of this alone. Remember, the Christian life is all about community. We recommend that you obtain an accountability partner or partners. They can be someone in the group, which may be preferable

because they have shared the same experience as you. Or it can be someone else, in which case you will have to explain to them what you have learned (see number 1 above) and share with them your plan for change (see number 2 above). Set up visits with your partner(s) to share with them your progress. Repetition and reinforcement are keys to changing habits. Stick with it and don't be discouraged if you are not initially successful. You can make these changes if you persevere.

Even if you didn't know it until now, God has been chasing you. He has been chasing you for a long time. Is it time for you to catch Him?

Finally, we offer this prayer. You may wish to use it or something similar to start your new journey. In either case, prayer is the line of communication which connects us with God. Learn to pray and learn to listen for the answers. We promise, He will answer. His answer may be "Yes," "No," or "Wait." Whatever answer you receive, just know that He has your best interests at heart.

PRAYER TO RECEIVE JESUS

Lord Jesus, thank You for pursuing me and for wanting me. Thank You for being patient with me. I recognize You are a Holy God, I am a sinful person, and my sin has created a distance between us. Thank You for sending Jesus who loved me enough to die on the cross for my benefit. I desire to be in a right relationship with You, so I am opening the door to my heart and inviting You to come in. Help me to remain close to You and to follow You wherever Your Spirit leads me. Be the Lord of my life and the guardian for my soul. This I pray in the name of Jesus, the Christ. Amen.